The Shetland Pony

This edition published 2014 by Lomond Books Ltd
14 Freskyn Place, Broxburn, EH52 5NF
www.lomondbooks.com

Text © John Abernethy
Illustrations © Garry Thorburn

ISBN 9781842042519

Printed in China

Shona

The Shetland Pony

In the Highlands of Scotland,
near the village of Dunguid,
and at the foot of the Beinn Aigh Hill,
there was a farm called Glen Millarbann.

And on this farm lived Mr & Mrs McDavies and their children, Ella and Robbie.

On the McDavies farm there were sheep, Highland cows, and some chickens. And a large poly-tunnel where Mr and Mrs McDavies grew all sorts of fruit and vegetables.

Every day, Mr and Mrs McDavies worked on the farm,
and every day Ella and Robbie helped
by feeding the sheep and collecting the eggs.

Ella and Robbie liked living on the farm with all the animals nearby.
But they also liked playing with their friends from the village,
Rory and Ewen, and Ilona and Amy -
who were always causing mischief.

One summer's day, Mr & Mrs McDavies told Ella and Robbie there was a surprise for them outside.
What could it be? A bicycle? A trampoline?

Ella and Robbie ran out of the house as fast as they could, and there they saw the prettiest Shetland pony they had ever seen!

What a surprise! The pony was brown,
but with a white fringe of hair that came down to her eyes.
Ella and Robbie were delighted.

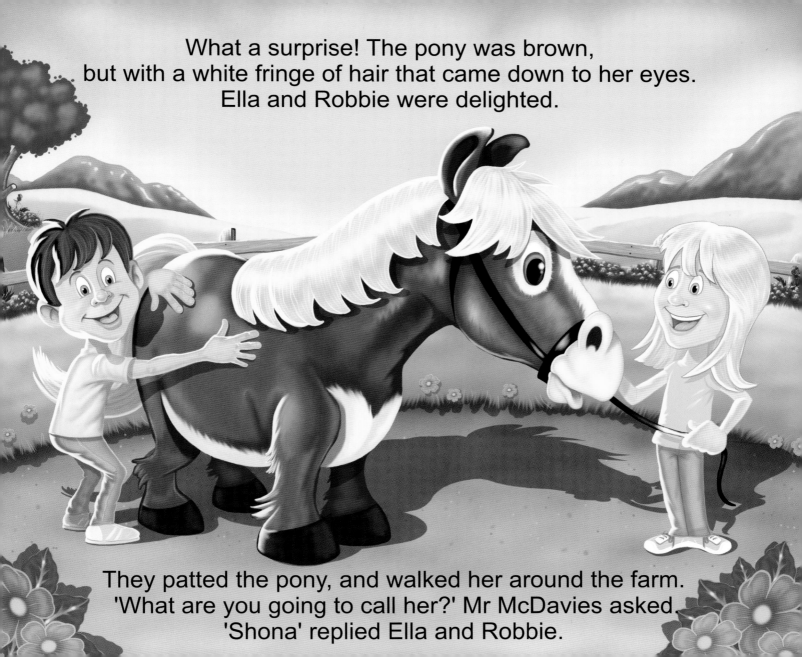

They patted the pony, and walked her around the farm.
'What are you going to call her?' Mr McDavies asked.
'Shona' replied Ella and Robbie.

All summer long, Ella and Robbie and Shona were inseparable.
They went for walks. They went for rides.

All the children from the village came to visit.
Shona was very happy in her new home.

At the end of the summer, Ella and Robbie went back to school.
Shona waited patiently in her field,
but some days Ella and Robbie did not come to see her at all.

Finn the Collie came to see Shona.
'Hello Shona. Do you want to play?' asked Finn.

Shona shook her head. 'No thanks Finn.
I am waiting for Ella and Robbie'.
But Ella and Robbie never came to visit that day.

As summer turned into autumn, the days became colder and darker,
and Shona's hair began to grow longer.
One day it rained and rained and then rained some more,
but Shona waited patiently for Ella and Robbie.

'Hello Shona' said Layla the Lamb.
'Do you want to find some shelter in the barn?'
Shona was soaked through, but she shook her head.
'Thank you Layla, but I am waiting for Ella and Robbie'.
But Ella and Robbie never came to visit that day.

As autumn turned into winter, snow began to fall on the farm, and Shona was covered from head to foot in snowflakes.

But Shona waited patiently for Ella and Robbie.

'Hello Shona' said Rosa the Robin.
'It is too cold to stay out here, you should go to the barn'.
Shona was shivering and her hair was nearly frozen,
but she shook her head.
'Thank you Rosa, but I am waiting for Ella and Robbie'.
But Ella and Robbie never came to visit that day.

Finally, a great storm hit the farm. Shona's hair was now very long indeed and was blowing everywhere in the wind

but still Shona waited patiently for Ella and Robbie

Hello Shona' said Heather the Highland cow.
You will be blown away if you stay out here! let's go to the barn'.

Shona did not want to go,
but Heather was very kind
and very wise and so Shona
followed Heather to the barn.

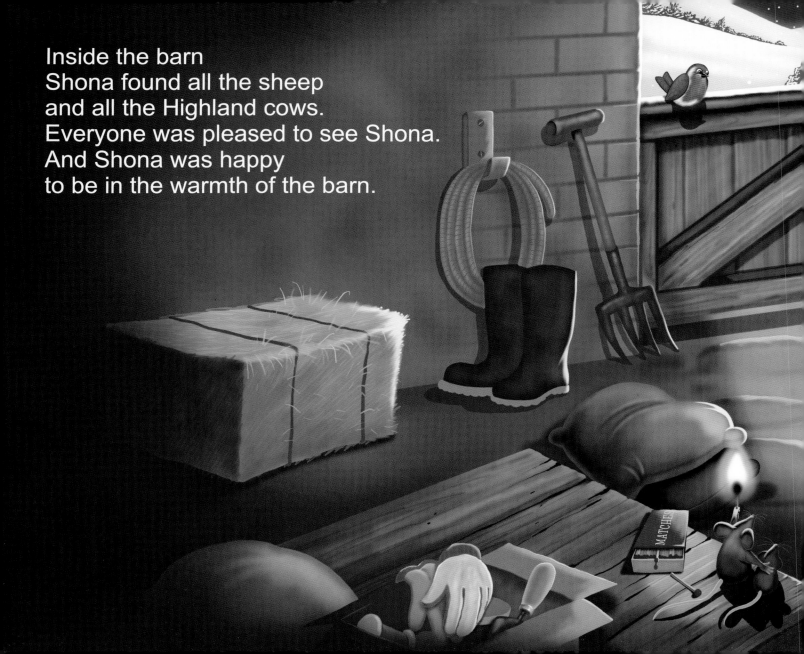

Inside the barn
Shona found all the sheep
and all the Highland cows.
Everyone was pleased to see Shona.
And Shona was happy
to be in the warmth of the barn.

In the spring the sun began to shine and the days became warmer. Shona played in the field with Heather and Layla and Finn and Rosa. Shona was very happy.

Although her hair was now so long that she could hardly see!

One sunny day,
Ella and Robbie finally came to see Shona,
but Shona kept running away.
Ella and Robbie did not understand
why Shona did not want to play,
and they felt very sad.

'Why won't Shona play with us?' they asked their mother.
Mrs McDavies smiled.
'You can't be friends only when the sun shines' she said.

Ella and Robbie bowed their heads.
They had not been good friends to Shona.

Ella and Robbie wanted to make things better.
The next day they brought Shona a Fair Isle blanket
for when the weather was cold.

And a pair of scissors to trim Shona's very long hair.
Shona was very pleased as she could see properly again!

Ella and Robbie had learned their lesson and went to see Shona every day. Shona was always so happy to see Ella and Robbie, but she was also happy to see Finn and Layla and Rosa and Heather.

Because no matter the weather,
you should always make time for your friends.

THE END